TIDY TITCH

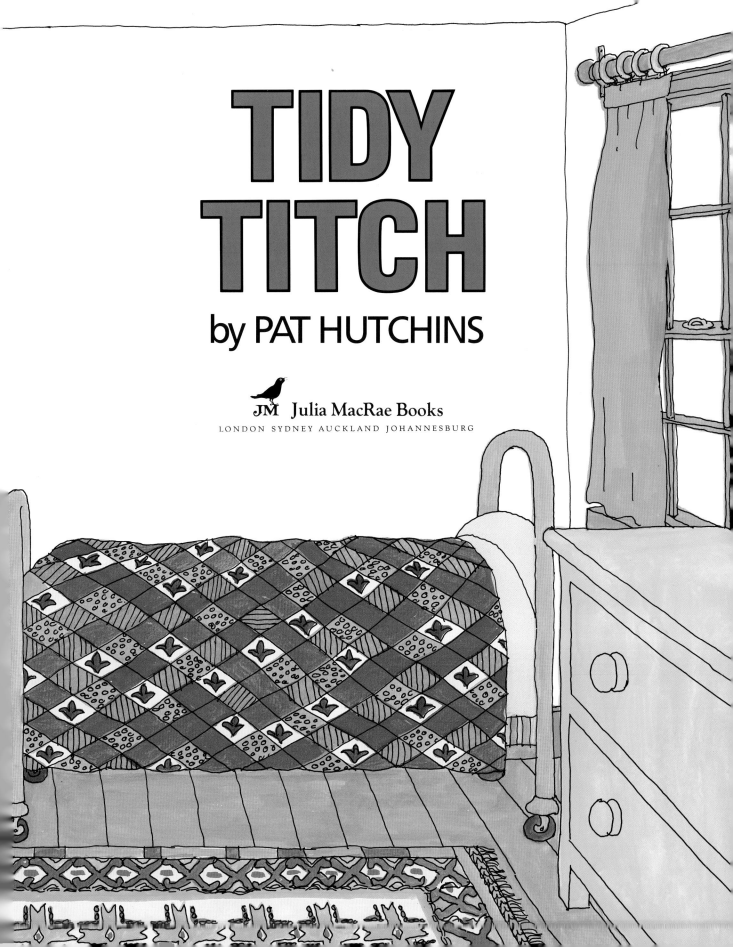

TIDY TITCH

by PAT HUTCHINS

JM Julia MacRae Books

LONDON SYDNEY AUCKLAND JOHANNESBURG

Copyright © 1991 Pat Hutchins
All rights reserved
First published in the USA 1991
by Greenwillow Books
First published in Great Britain 1991
by Julia MacRae
a division of Random House UK Ltd
20 Vauxhall Bridge Road, London SW1V 2SA

Random House Australia (Pty) Ltd
20 Alfred Street, Milsons Point, Sydney, NSW 2061

Random House New Zealand Ltd
18 Poland Road, Glenfield, Auckland 10, New Zealand

Random House South Africa (Pty) Ltd
PO Box 337, Bergvlei, 2012, South Africa

Printed in Hong Kong

Reprinted 1992, 1993, 1994, 1998

British Library Cataloguing in Publication Data
Hutchins, Pat *1942-*
Tidy titch.
I. Title
823.914[J]
ISBN 1-85681-151-4

FOR DAISY GOUNDRY

TIDY TITCH

"How tidy Titch's room is,"
said Mother to Peter and Mary.
"And how messy your rooms are.
I think you should tidy them up."

"I'll help," said Titch
as Mother went downstairs.

"I think I'll throw this
dolls' house out," said Mary,
"and these toys.
I'm too old for them!"
"I'm not," said Titch.
"I'll have them!"

And Titch carried the dolls' house
and the toys to his room.

"I think I'll throw that old
space suit out," said Peter,
"and that cowboy outfit.
They're much too small for me!"
"They're not too small for me!"
said Titch. "I'll have them!"

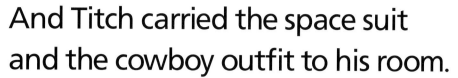

And Titch carried the space suit
and the cowboy outfit to his room.

"My room is still untidy," said Mary.
"I think I'll get rid of this broken pram
and these old games.
I've played them hundreds of times!"

"I haven't," said Titch.
"I'll have them!"

And Titch took the pram
and old games to his room.

"My room is still a mess," said Peter.
"I think I'll get rid of
    these old toys. I don't play
    with them any more!"
"I will!" said Titch.
"I'll have them!"

And Titch carried the old toys to his room.

"How neat your rooms are!" said Mother
when she came back upstairs.

"I thought Titch was going to help you."

"He did," said Peter and Mary.

Since the publication of *Rosie's Walk* in 1968, reviewers on both sides of the Atlantic have been loud in their praise of Pat Hutchins's work.

Among her popular picture books are *What Game Shall We Play?*; *Where's the Baby?*; *The Doorbell Rang*; *Titch*; and *The Wind Blew* (Winner of the 1974 Kate Greenaway Medal). For older readers she has written several novels, including *The House That Sailed Away, The Curse of the Egyptian Mummy* and *Rats!*

Pat Hutchins, her husband, Laurence, and their sons, Morgan and Sam, live in London.